D0236134

1 3 5 7 9 10 8 6 4 2
ISBN: 978-0-00-751996-5
First published by HarperCollins *Children's Books* in 2013.

Text by Paddy Kempshall

The Hobbit: The Desolation of Smaug Annual 2014 is a companion to the film *The Hobbit: The Desolation of Smaug* and is published with the permission, but not the approval, of the Estate of the late J.R.R. Tolkien. Dialogue quotations are from the film, not the novel.

The Hobbit is published by HarperCollinsPublishers under licence from The Trustees of The J.R.R. Tolkien Estate Limited.

Printed and bound in Italy

THE HOBBIT™
THE DESOLATION OF SMAUG
Annual 2014

HarperCollins *Children's Books*

CONTENTS

THE COMPANY

If you want to join Bilbo and his companions on their quest to the Lonely Mountain, it would be best if you knew a little something about them!

GANDALF THE GREY
One of the most powerful Wizards in the whole of Middle-earth, Gandalf is wise and cunning. While he is helping Thorin with his mission, Gandalf is also a member of the White Council, and has quests of his own to fulfil.

GANDALF THE GREY

BOMBUR

BIFUR

DORI

BOFUR

KILI

BOFUR, BOMBUR AND BIFUR
This family of Dwarves sometimes seems to have more in common with hobbits, which is why they get along with Bilbo so well. Bofur is always looking for fun and his good humour is infectious. Bombur is The Company's cook and if he's not cooking food, he's eating it. Or thinking about eating it… With a rusting piece of an Orc's axe stuck in his forehead, Bifur is a sight to scare even the bravest of foes. What makes him even scarier is that Bifur can't talk and can only communicate through grunting and waving his hands!

THORIN OAKENSHIELD
A strong and fearless fighter, Thorin is the leader of The Company. His family once ruled the area around the Lonely Mountain, until the Dragon Smaug drove them from their homes.

DORI, NORI AND ORI
The youngest of the three brothers, Ori is a great artist and also keeps a journal about The Company's adventures. Dori always thinks the worst is going to happen, but that never stops him trying his hardest. As the member of the family usually getting into trouble, Nori doesn't always get on with his brothers, but he will never let them down.

FILI AND KILI

Raised in the far-off Blue Mountains, these two young Dwarves have joined their uncle Thorin on his quest. Fili is a skilled fighter and his brother, Kili, is an expert with a bow. They have never travelled far until now, and have little idea of the dangers that lie ahead.

OIN AND GLOIN

Brothers Oin and Gloin are also distant relations of Thorin. Oin is the healer of the group and can make many medicines from herbs. Gloin has a temper almost as wild as his beard. Extremely strong and outspoken, he often has little thought for the consequences of his actions.

IORIN OAKENSHIELD

DWALIN

BILBO BAGGINS

BALIN

FILI

NORI

GLOIN

ORI

OIN

BALIN

A Dwarf Lord, Balin is old and wise. He is one of Thorin's closest friends and advisers, and is always willing to listen and offer some wise counsel. Balin is distantly related to Thorin, and is a descendant of the noble house of Durin.

BILBO BAGGINS

A hobbit from the Shire, Bilbo is an unlikely hero on a very unexpected journey! Not normally one for having adventures, Bilbo has found himself hired by Thorin to be the group's burglar and help them in their quest!

DWALIN

Tall, moody, strong and very brave, Dwalin is a Dwarf through and through. A famous warrior and a powerful ally, Dwalin would like nothing more than to see the return of the Dwarven King under the Mountain.

THE JOURNEY SO FAR

Bilbo's quest with The Company has already been a long and dangerous journey.
Read on to find out about the wonderful sights and terrible enemies he has already faced.

One fine morning, Bilbo Baggins was sitting outside his home in the Shire when the legendary Wizard, Gandalf the Grey invited him to share in an adventure. Being a sensible hobbit, Bilbo politely refused to be part of such a disturbing notion as an adventure, went into his house and thought no more about it.

Later that evening, he was visited by 13 rather loud and extremely hairy Dwarves; Dwalin, Balin, Fili, Kili, Oin, Gloin, Ori, Dori, Nori, Bofur, Bombur, Bifur and their leader, Thorin Oakenshield. While the Dwarves made themselves at home and ate all of Bilbo's food, Gandalf and Thorin explained their quest.

Long ago, a great Dwarven King ruled at the Lonely Mountain, Erebor. One day, consumed by greed for the Dwarves' gold, a savage Dragon called Smaug attacked the mountain and drove the Dwarven King and his people out of his realm. The King's name was Thrór and he was Thorin's grandfather. Now, Thorin and his companions are determined to recover his family's treasure from Smaug, but they need a burglar to help them.

Unfortunately for Bilbo, Gandalf was determined that he was just the hobbit for the job! So, the next morning he found himself riding off into the mountains with them on a very unexpected journey!

On their first night, Bilbo and his companions had some of their ponies stolen in the dark. As The Company's burglar, Bilbo felt he ought to go and see what had happened to them. Creeping through the darkness he was very surprised to see that they had been stolen by three huge Trolls!

Bilbo and his friends were caught by the Trolls and stuffed into sacks! Luckily, Bilbo had a clever idea – he made the Trolls argue about how they were going to cook and eat their prisoners, so they didn't notice that the sun was rising. From out of the shadows, Gandalf appeared and split open a rock that was shading the trolls from sunlight.

As the rays of the sun fell over the Trolls they turned to stone, and Bilbo and his companions were saved!

After they escaped from the Trolls, Bilbo and The Company found the Trolls' hideout. Inside the hidden cave, Thorin and Gandalf discovered three very special swords. Gandalf gave the smallest of the swords to Bilbo, which he took reluctantly – hobbits don't like to fight, but Gandalf knew that Bilbo would need protection.

But as they left the cave, the group realised they weren't as safe as they thought! A terrible howl filled the air as a vicious pack of Wargs jumped forward to attack them. Fighting bravely, the Dwarves managed to kill two of the vicious beasts, but more closed in on them.

Gandalf realised that trying to escape was their best option, so he led The Company into the foothills of the Misty Mountains, with the Wargs gaining on them with every step! But as things looked bleak for Bilbo and his friends, Gandalf led them into a hidden valley within the rocks.

The Company had entered Rivendell – the secret and magical home of the Elves. Gandalf's old friend, Elrond, welcomed the group and offered them a place to rest. That night, Elrond translated the mystical moon runes on Thorin's map – revealing a secret door in the Lonely Mountain that would lead them into the lair of the Dragon, Smaug.

During their time at Rivendell, Gandalf also learned that another ancient enemy had returned to Middle-earth. It was something far more powerful and evil than Smaug, and could not be ignored. So, while The Company slipped away from Rivendell to continue their quest, Gandalf instead headed south on an adventure of his own.

Bilbo and his companions pressed on higher into the Misty Mountains. As a huge storm gathered, The Company took shelter in a cave. With the winds howling around them, Bofur kept watch as his friends huddled down.

Bilbo began to fear that he was not the hobbit for this quest after all, and decided that The Company would be better off without him. Just as Bofur was convincing him to stay, the floor of the cave suddenly dropped away and the group were plunged into the inky depths below. Tumbling into the dark caves, Bilbo and his friends eventually came crashing to a halt inside a rusty cage. They had been captured by Goblins!

While The Company were being led away through the dark caves, Bilbo managed to slip away from the Goblins into a gloomy side-tunnel. But just as Bilbo thought that his escape had gone unnoticed, a Goblin pounced out of the shadows and started chasing him!

Poor Bilbo couldn't run fast enough and soon the Goblin had him in his grasp. Struggling and fighting, they fell into a dark crevasse – even further into the depths of the mountains.

Luckily, the Goblin was knocked out by the fall – but that left Bilbo alone and afraid in the dark. Stumbling blindly through the shadows, Bilbo found a plain gold ring in the dirt. Without thinking, he popped it into his pocket and pressed on to the shores of an underground lake.

Here, he came face to face with a shrunken, shrivelled creature called Gollum, who was hungry for hobbit. After betting his life for freedom, Bilbo defeated Gollum in a riddle contest and forced him to show him the way out of the caves. But the ring Bilbo had found was Gollum's, and when he realised Bilbo had it in his pocket, he flew into an uncontrollable rage! He attacked Bilbo and chased him into the tunnels.

Meanwhile, Thorin and the other Dwarves had been dragged in front of the fearsome and grotesque Goblin King. After they bravely refused to tell the King anything about their quest, they were sentenced to death!

But as the Goblins closed in, Gandalf returned in a blinding flash of light. Leaping into battle, Gandalf struck down the King and set his friends free. Taking advantage of the confusion, Thorin and the Dwarves escaped into the caverns.

Meanwhile, Bilbo was still trying to escape Gollum. By accident, Bilbo ended up wearing the ring he had found – and discovered he had become invisible! Using the magic ring, he escaped and was reunited with his friends once more.

But the danger wasn't over and soon the group were chased by a pack of Orcs and Wargs. They climbed trees to try and escape the snapping fangs and while the vicious beasts tried to reach them, Gandalf captured a moth and sent a secret message.

Then he cast a spell on some pine cones and flung them at the animals below. The cones exploded in a shower of flames and set fire to everything around them – including the trees Bilbo and his friends were hiding in!

With everyone huddled in the last tree still standing, things looked grim. But suddenly a group of Great Eagles arrived, summoned by Gandalf's message, and swept The Company off into the sky and safety.

Now Bilbo's journey continues...

TATTERED AND TORN

Thorin's map has been damaged in a battle and is full of holes! Draw a line to place the pieces that have fallen out into the correct spaces to complete the map.

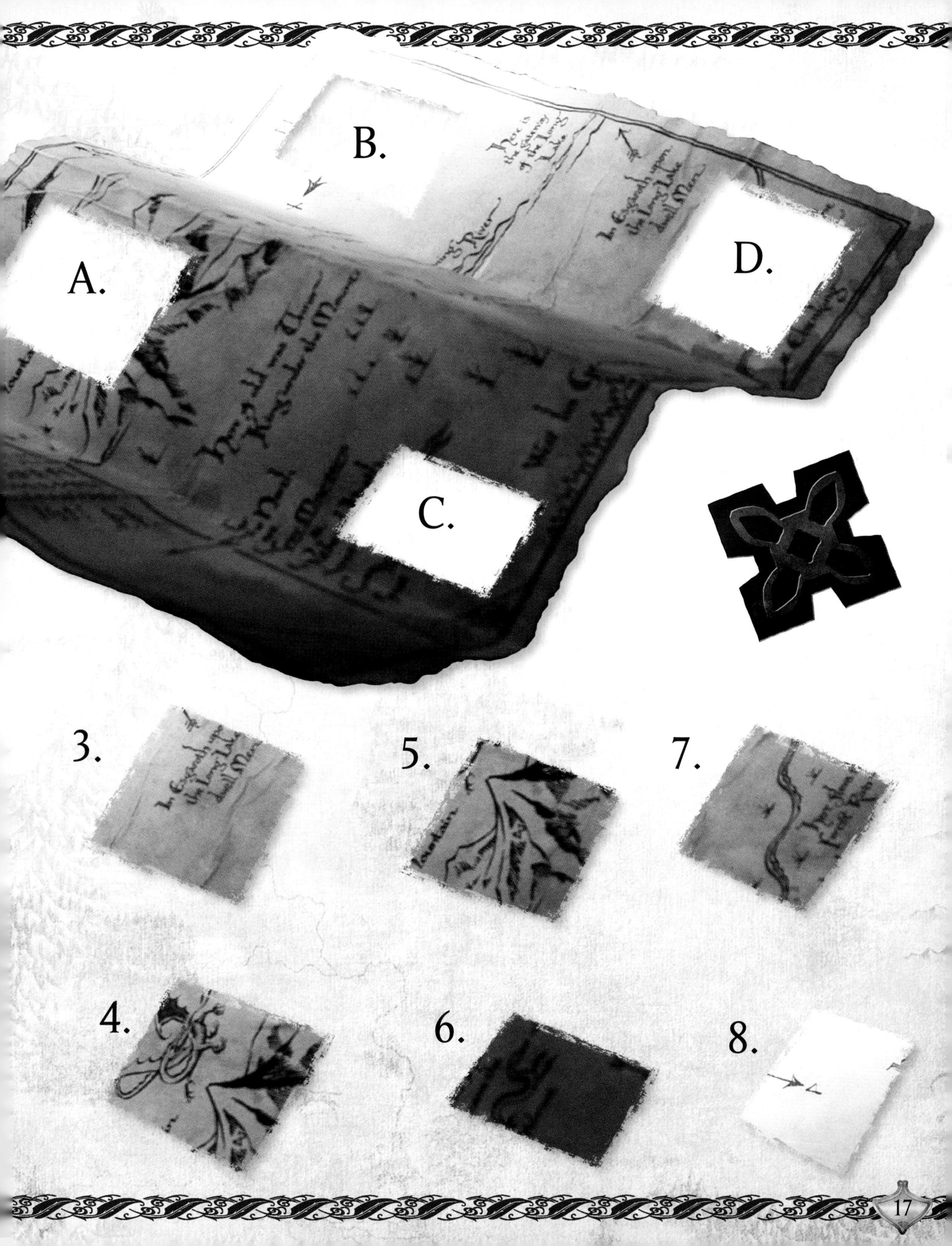
A.
B.
C.
D.
3.
4.
5.
6.
7.
8.

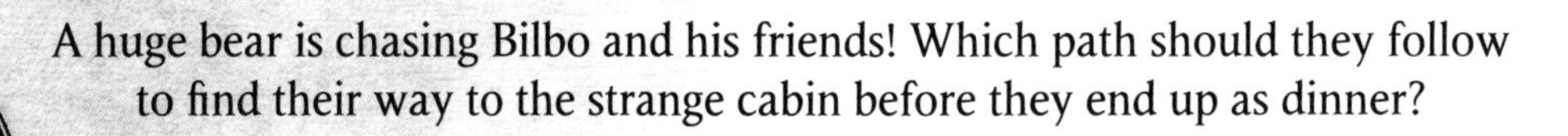

A huge bear is chasing Bilbo and his friends! Which path should they follow to find their way to the strange cabin before they end up as dinner?

INSTRUCTIONS

Move in the direction of the arrow.

Move the number of spaces shown.

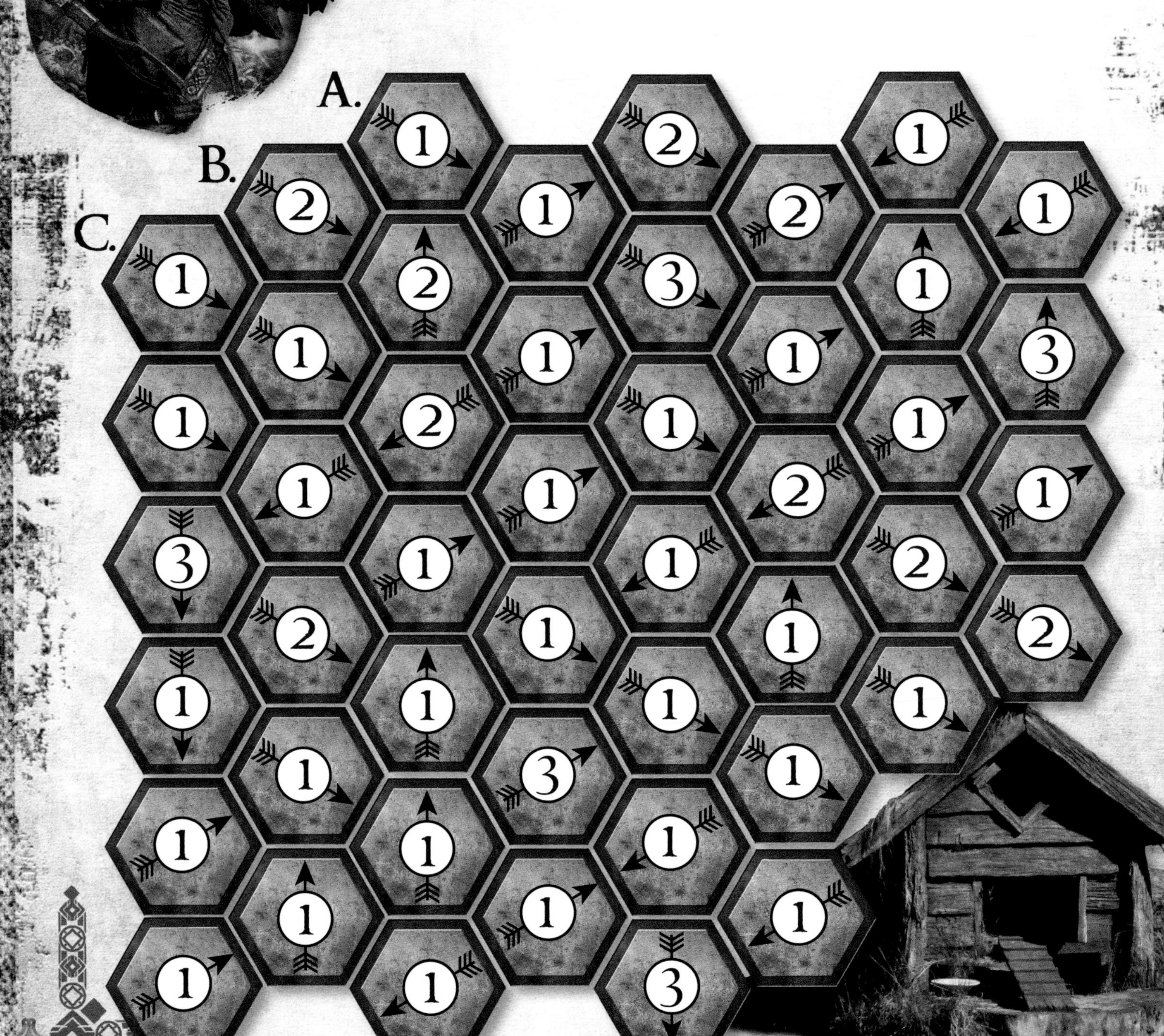

RUNE WHEEL

Nori has found a mysterious message in Beorn's cabin.
Follow the instructions to help him decode it.

INSTRUCTIONS

Follow the circle in a clockwise direction. Use the key to translate every third rune and write the letters in the spaces to read the message. We've circled the first letter for you.

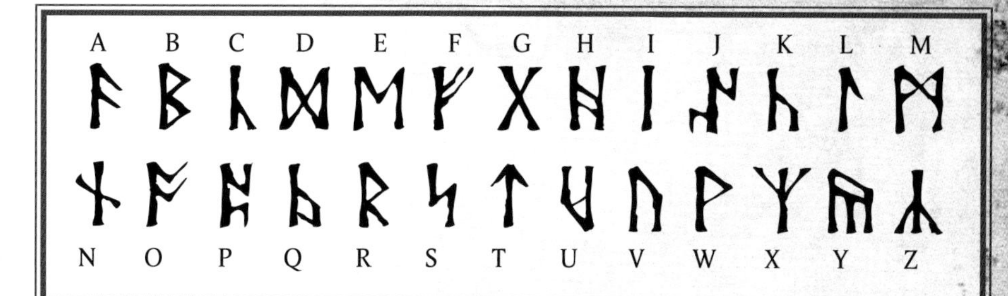

ANSWER

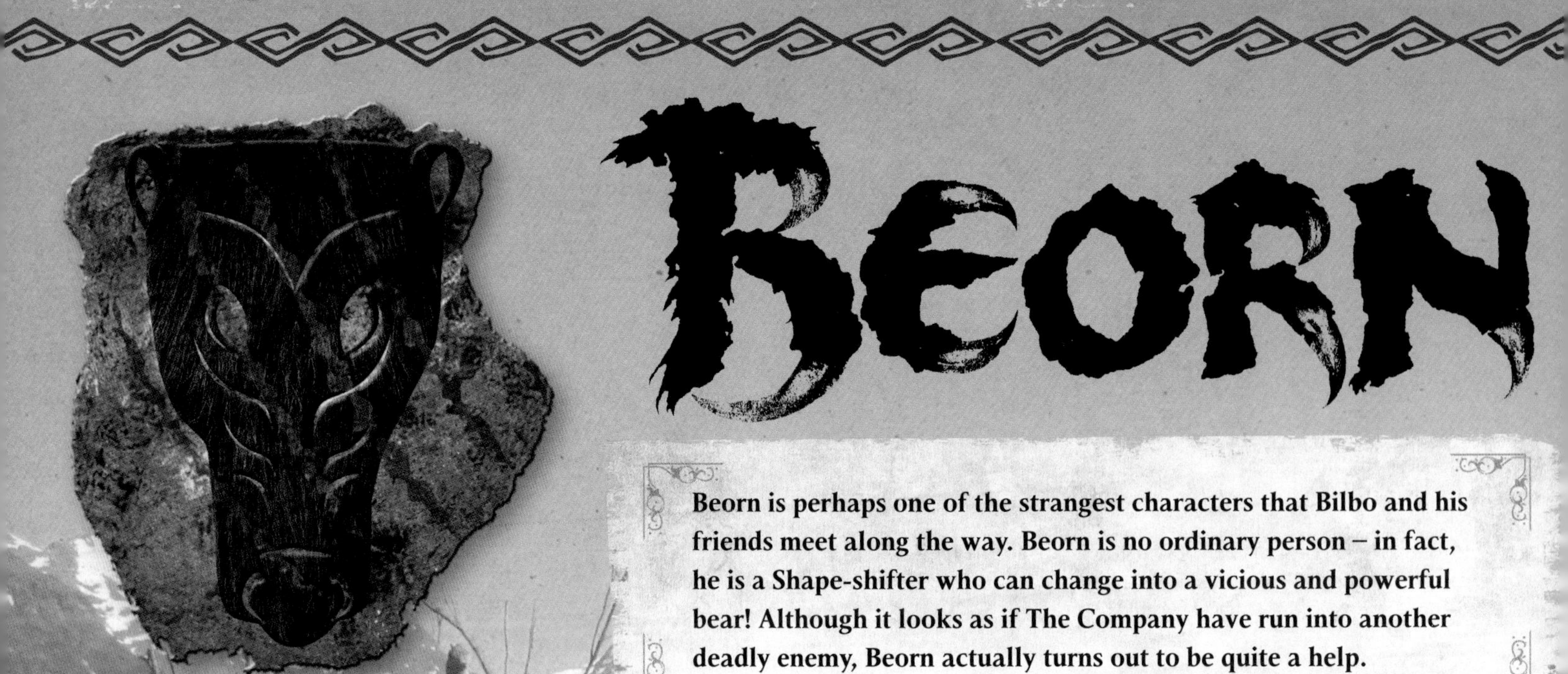

BEORN

Beorn is perhaps one of the strangest characters that Bilbo and his friends meet along the way. Beorn is no ordinary person – in fact, he is a Shape-shifter who can change into a vicious and powerful bear! Although it looks as if The Company have run into another deadly enemy, Beorn actually turns out to be quite a help.

Living in a wooden and stone house behind a large hedge, Beorn really doesn't like strangers, especially Dwarves!

DID YOU KNOW?

Beorn keeps lots of bees and makes very tasty honey!

Beorn is the last Shape-shifter in the whole of Middle-earth. Most of his kind were killed by Azog, so when Beorn finds out that The Company are fleeing from Azog, he agrees to help them. As well as giving Bilbo and his friends somewhere safe to rest, Beorn also gives them information. He lets Gandalf know that the rumours of a great evil rising in the south are true, and makes him realise that his own quest is just as important as Thorin's. He also warns The Company about travelling through Mirkwood.

THE WONDROUS WORLD

Bilbo's travels with Thorin and the rest of The Company have taken him far from his home in the Shire. From towering mountains to cavernous depths, the heroes find themselves passing through some truly amazing places.

BEORN'S CABIN

When the group are searching for somewhere to rest after their dangerous journey through the Misty Mountains, Gandalf leads them here. But after they are chased by a huge bear, Bilbo thinks that they might have been safer if they'd stayed up a tree surrounded by Wargs! However, the Shape-shifter Beorn reveals that he is the bear and welcomes everyone into his home. The Company are able to rest here in peace before continuing their quest.

MIRKWOOD

When Gandalf heads south on a quest of his own, The Company are faced with travelling through this weird wood on their own. Blanketed in shadows and filled with decay and evil, Mirkwood has claimed the lives of many an unwary traveller. If the deadly waters of its dark rivers don't claim you, then one of the horrible creatures lurking in the shadows surely will…

THE HALL OF THE ELVENKING

The fortress of Thranduil, the King of the Wood Elves. Thranduil sees Mirkwood as his private realm and has little patience for those who enter it without his permission – especially if they happen to be Dwarves. Built over the swift river that leads to the Long Lake, it is here that Thorin and his companions are taken when they are captured by the Elves. Luckily for them, Bilbo has a trick or two up his sleeve.

LAKE-TOWN

Once a bustling and lively trading town, Lake-town was devastated by the Dragon Smaug when he drove the Dwarves from the Lonely Mountain. It's now a dying, rotting town... and it really smells of fish! The Master is the head of Lake-town. He is their mayor, lawyer and leader all rolled into one. He may seem to be an honourable man, who has the best interests of the people of Lake-town at heart, but things aren't always what they seem. He is helped by a very creepy man called Alfrid. In fact, Alfrid is as much the Master's slave as his helper, and would do anything for him.

DOL GULDUR

Far to the south, Dol Guldur is the site of the ancient ruins of an abandoned fortress. It was here that Radagast found evidence that a great evil had returned to Middle-earth, an evil more powerful and dangerous than even Smaug. Warned by this, Gandalf goes there to investigate if the rumours of the Necromancer's return are true.

THE LONELY MOUNTAIN

For many years, Erebor was the home of the Dwarven King Under the Mountain, until Smaug drove out the Dwarves and scattered them across Middle-earth. It is to here that Thorin and his companions are travelling, hoping to slay the Dragon and reclaim the Kingdom and its riches. According to Thorin's map, there is a hidden door far up in the slopes of the mountain that can give them access to the caverns below.

PICK A PART

Where would you fit into Bilbo's tale? Follow the paths and answer the questions to find out which character you are most like.

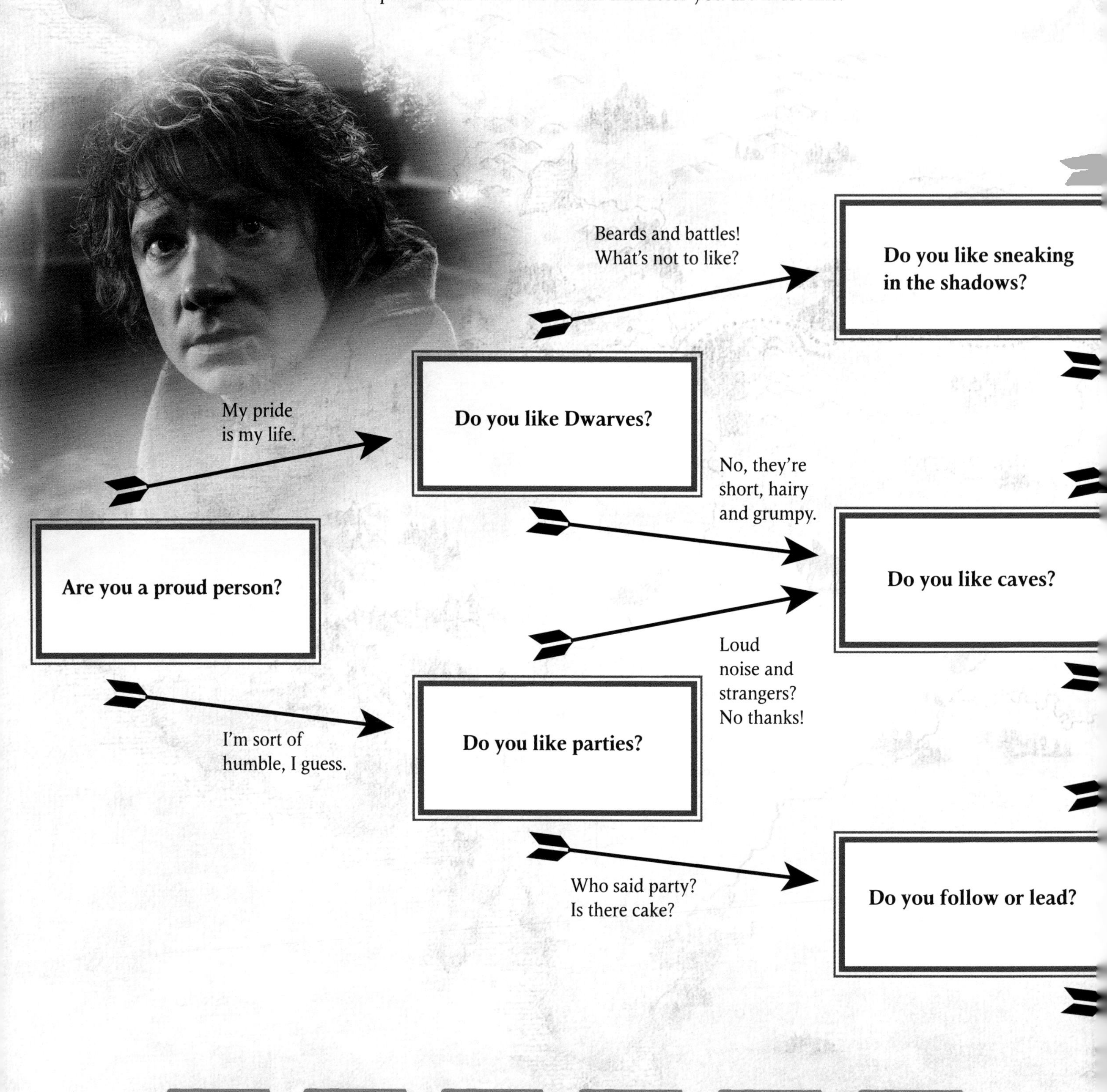

Are you a proud person?
My pride is my life.
I'm sort of humble, I guess.
Do you like Dwarves?
Beards and battles! What's not to like?
No, they're short, hairy and grumpy.
Do you like parties?
Loud noise and strangers? No thanks!
Who said party? Is there cake?
Do you like sneaking in the shadows?
Do you like caves?
Do you follow or lead?

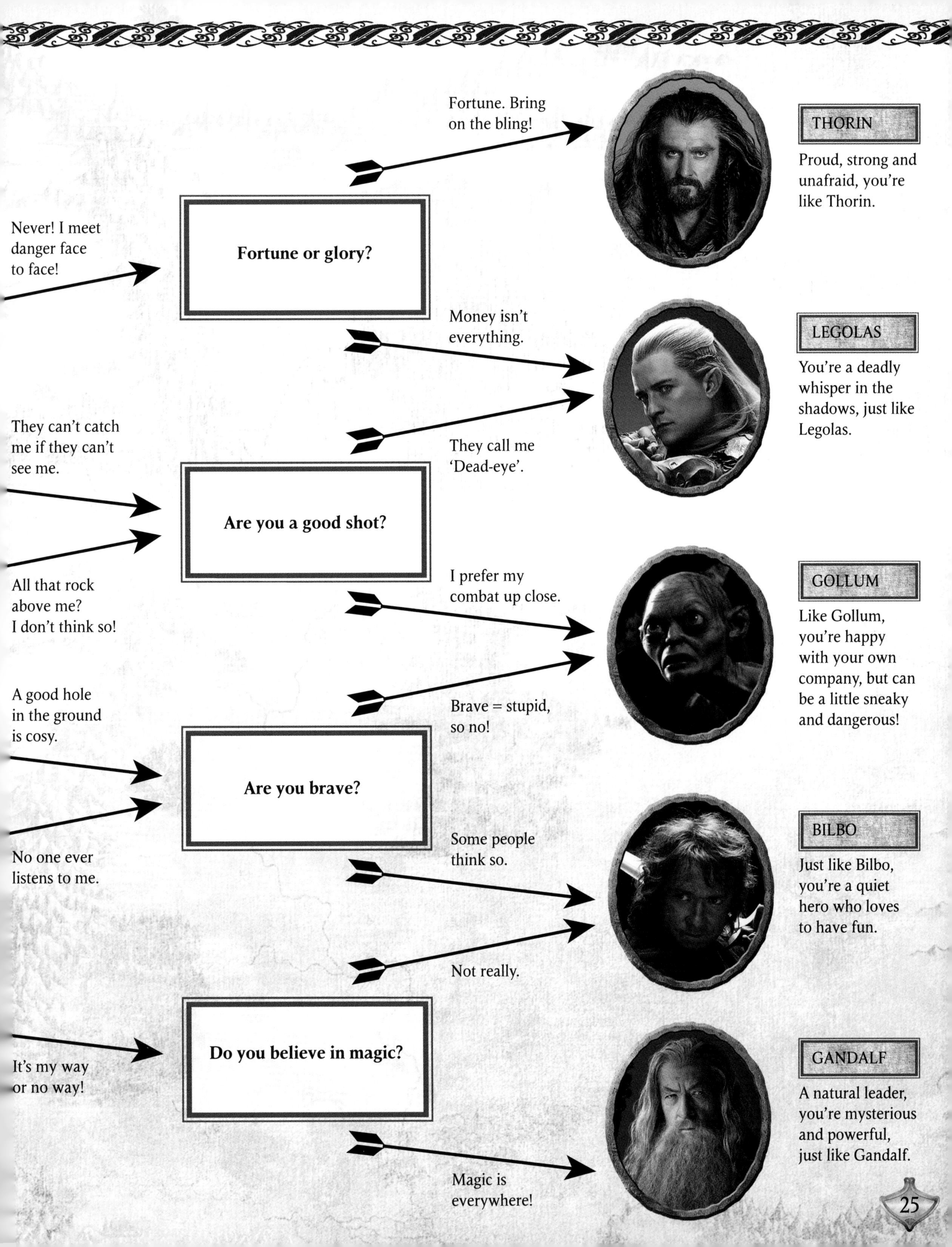
Never! I meet danger face to face!
Fortune or glory?
Fortune. Bring on the bling!
Money isn't everything.
THORIN
Proud, strong and unafraid, you're like Thorin.
They can't catch me if they can't see me.
All that rock above me? I don't think so!
Are you a good shot?
They call me 'Dead-eye'.
I prefer my combat up close.
LEGOLAS
You're a deadly whisper in the shadows, just like Legolas.
A good hole in the ground is cosy.
No one ever listens to me.
Are you brave?
Brave = stupid, so no!
Some people think so.
Not really.
GOLLUM
Like Gollum, you're happy with your own company, but can be a little sneaky and dangerous!
It's my way or no way!
Do you believe in magic?
Magic is everywhere!
BILBO
Just like Bilbo, you're a quiet hero who loves to have fun.
GANDALF
A natural leader, you're mysterious and powerful, just like Gandalf.

RUNE REMEDIES

Can you help Oin complete his ancient recipes?

INSTRUCTIONS

Fill in the grids so that each row, column and small 2x2 square contain one of each rune.

Radagast

Although he commands powerful magic like Gandalf, there isn't much else that is similar about these two great Wizards! Forgetful, easily distracted and quite eccentric, Radagast is more comfortable talking to animals than he is to people and can often be found wandering through the woodlands all over Middle-earth.

Also known as Radagast the Brown, he is one of the guardians of the great forests of Middle-earth. He is one of the first to notice the evil and decay that is falling on Mirkwood and is also the first to find out that the Necromancer has returned to Dol Guldur!

DID YOU KNOW?

Radagast lives in the forest in a place called Rhosgobel.

It was Radagast who handed Gandalf a Morgul blade that he had found at Dol Guldur, proving that the rise of an ancient evil was indeed happening there.

While he may seem absent-minded and odd, Radagast is a brave and powerful ally. When Thorin and his friends are attacked by a vicious pack of Wargs, it is Radagast who bravely draws them away so that The Company can escape and continue on their quest.

SPIDER SEARCH

The Dwarves have been captured by the Mirkwood spiders! Bilbo has freed himself, but can you help him find his way to his friends without running into any more spiders?

FINISH

MIRKWOOD MUDDLERS

Bilbo's friends are about to be a spider's lunch! Can you help Bilbo solve these tricky puzzles and rescue his friends?

The power of 5

Help Bilbo sneak up on the spiders. The quietest path is to follow the leaves where the answer to the sums is less than 5. You can only go up, down or across.

START	1+3	21÷3	90÷30	45÷5	26-23	18-15	9÷3
4x2	10-6	18-12	24-17	60-54	40÷10	2×3	2+2
23-17	2x2	9-6	1x4	17-11	9-7	1+5	100÷25
40÷20	6+5	5+4	8÷2	30-26	21÷7	8÷1	3×1
3×9	11-6	22÷2	34-27	9-3	20÷2	14×2	FINISH

Shape-shifting

It's magic time – but Bilbo can't remember which pocket he put the Ring in! Use the code to add up the symbols on each pocket. The Ring is in the pocket with the highest number answer.

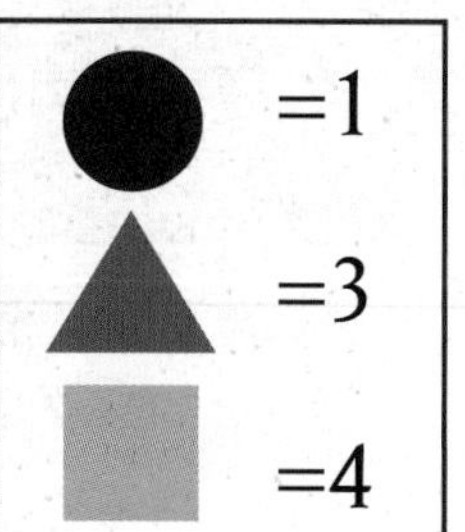

A.

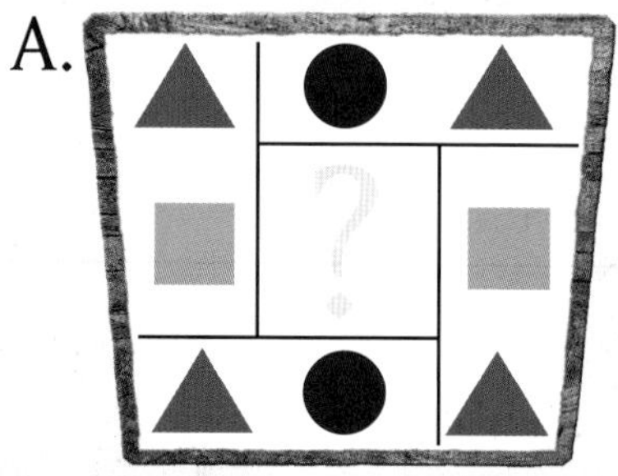

B.

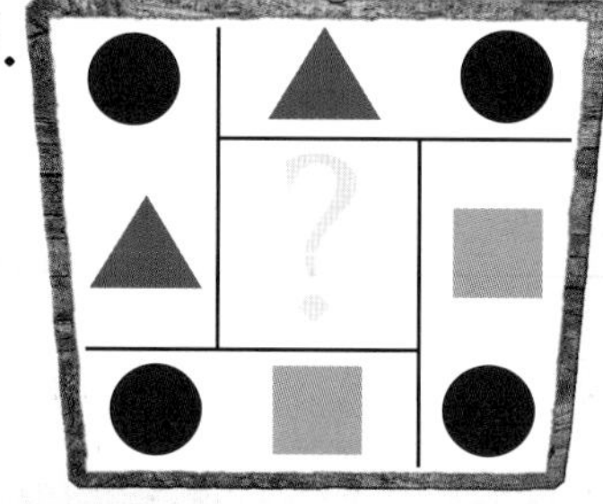

C.

D.

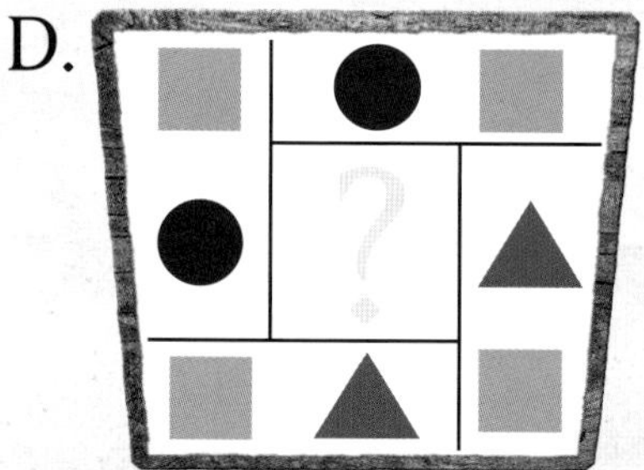

Number tree

Bilbo needs to climb into the trees to cut down the webs trapping his friends. Look at the number stack and see if you can work out the missing numbers to help Bilbo climb higher.

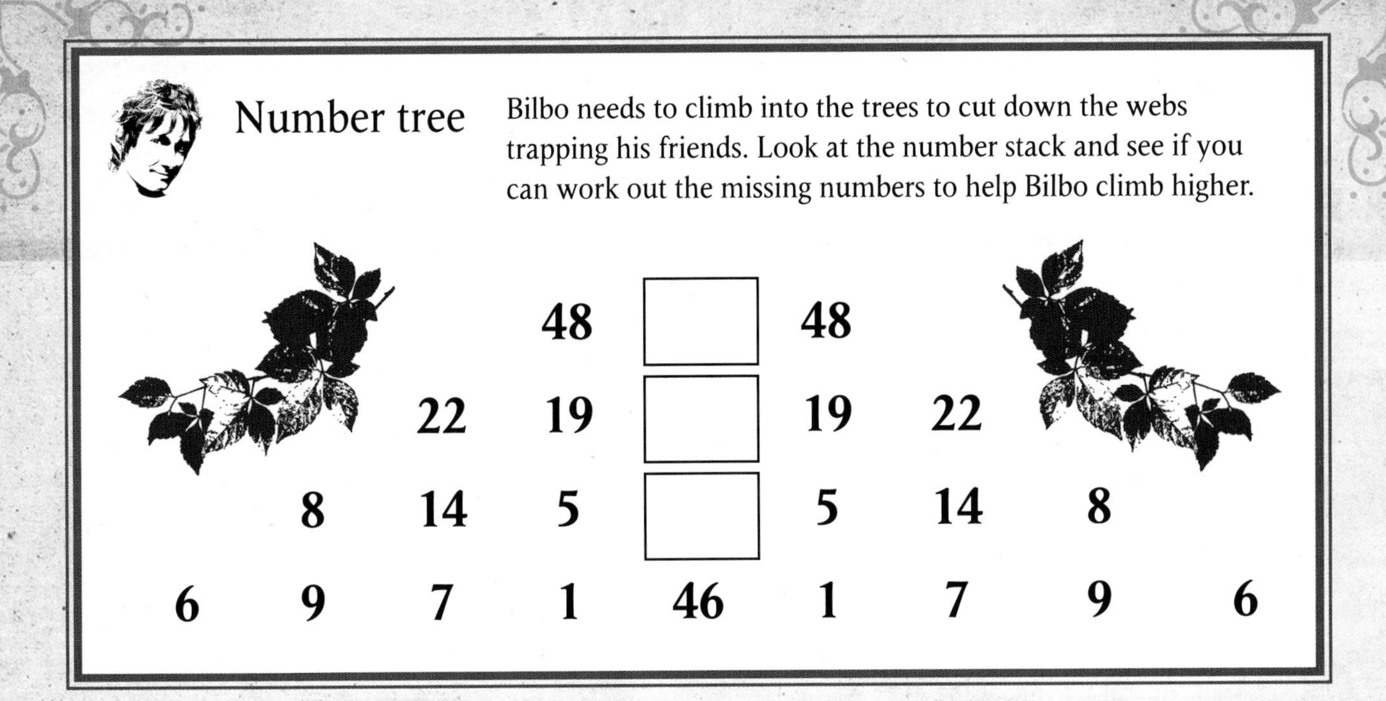

Take aim

Time to cause a distraction! Which stones should Bilbo throw to hit the spiders? The stones bounce off the diagonal walls. We've started stone A to show you how.

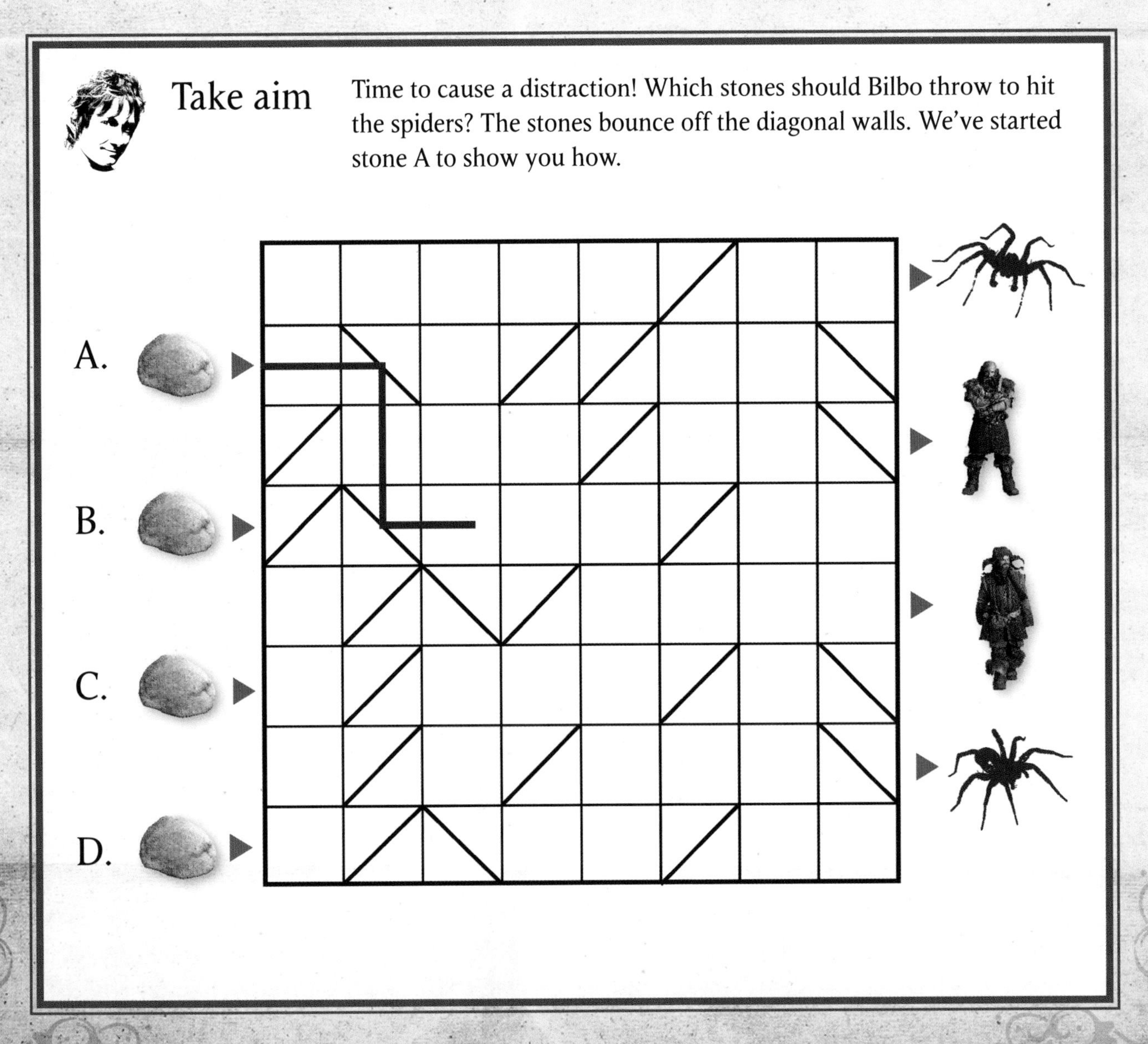

Thranduil

The King of the Wood Elves, Thranduil rules from a fortress deep in the heart of Mirkwood. He is very proud and does not look kindly on strangers wandering in his realm – especially if they happen to be Dwarves. Like all Elves, Thranduil has lived for a very long time and was near the Lonely Mountain when Smaug attacked it.

In fact Thranduil was ready with a huge army, but decided not to risk the lives of his forces. Thorin has never forgiven Thranduil for not helping when Smaug attacked and drove his ancestors out of their home.

DID YOU KNOW?

Thranduil's son is Legolas – a brave and highly skilled Elf who follows the Dwarves after they escape from Mirkwood.

When Thranduil captures Thorin and the rest of The Company, he guesses that they are on their way back to the Lonely Mountain to try and retake their kingdom. He tries to get Thorin to promise him some of Smaug's treasure in return for his release, but Thorin refuses.

Thranduil has ordered the Elves in his command to remain in Mirkwood and stay out of the affairs of others in Middle-earth. This has meant that they have gained a reputation for being a strange race with few friends, and many enemies!

where is Dain
Lonely
Mountain

DUNGEON RUNNER

Help guide The Company through the twisting tunnels of Thranduil's fortress to the wine cellar, so Bilbo can carry out his plan to escape!

START

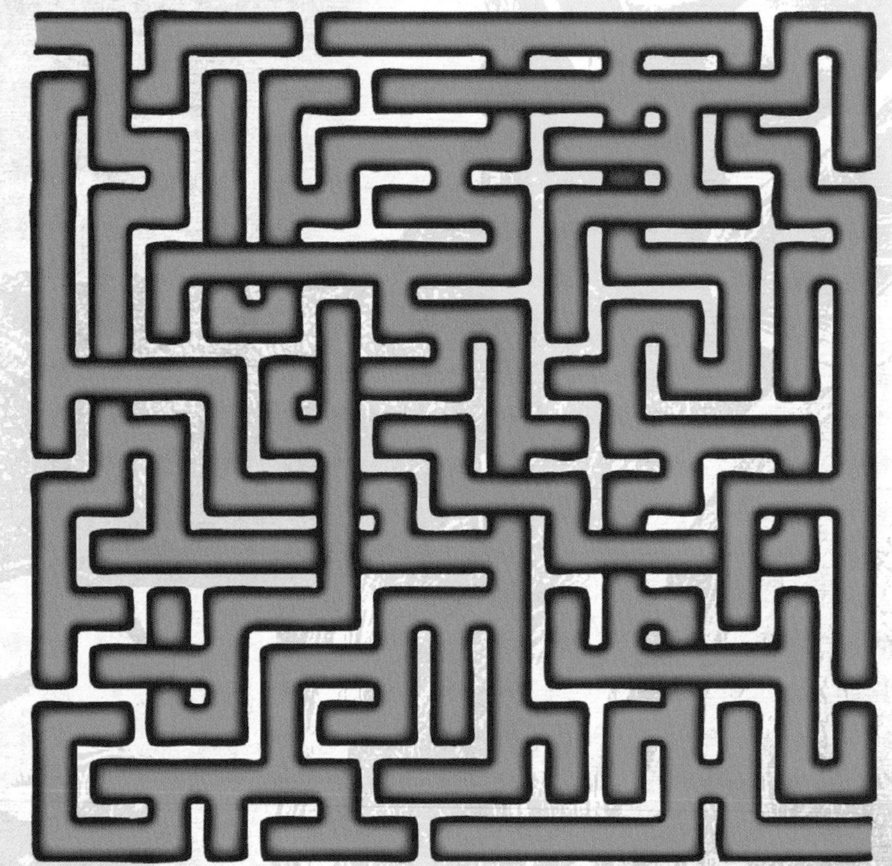

FINISH

Legolas

Legolas is a Wood Elf from Mirkwood and is the son of Thranduil, the King of the Wood Elves. He is known for being an exceptional shot with a bow, but is also extremely skilled when fighting with deadly Elven daggers.

Although he is Thranduil's son and the Prince of the Elves in Mirkwood, Legolas does not always see eye-to-eye with his father. While they both share the typical Elven mistrust of Dwarves, it seems that Legolas may not be as set in his ways as his father.

DID YOU KNOW?

Legolas' full name is Legolas Greenleaf

Legolas has amazing eyesight and can spot even the smallest targets at a much greater distance than a Dwarf or a man could see. He also has extremely good hearing and can move through forests without making a sound.

He is very protective of Tauriel and goes after her when she follows Bilbo and The Company out of the forest to Lake-town.

BARREL BOTHER

Bilbo has stuffed his friends into barrels so he can float them off down the river, but he can't remember who is in which barrel! Can you help?

SPOT THE DIFFERENCE

There are 6 differences between these pictures of Kili.
Can you spot them all? Circle them on the bottom picture.

A.

B.

RIVER ESCAPE

Dwarves

The Dwarves are floating away in their barrels, but Thranduil's Wood Elves are in hot pursuit! Can you escape down the river before they catch you?

Wood Elves

1. START

2.

3.

4.

5. Ow! You're tossed about by the waves and bang your head. Go back 1 space.

6.

7. **CRUNCH!** Look out! You've hit a rock. Move the Wood Elves on 1 space while you bail out the water.

8.

9. You've found a short cut! Hurry on 2 spaces.

10.

11.

RULES:

- Cut out or copy the two counters and place them both on the START.
- Roll a die and move the Dwarves' counter along the board, following any instructions you land on.
- After each turn, move the Wood Elves' counter TWO spaces along the board. (The Wood Elves don't need to follow any of the instructions on the board.)
- If the Wood Elves catch your counter before you reach the end, you've been captured again!

12\. They're firing arrows at you! Move the Wood Elves on 2 more spaces while you take cover.

13\.

14\.

15\. Great paddling. Move on 1 space as you race away from the Wood Elves.

16\.

17\.

18\.

19\. Where's Bilbo? Go back 2 spaces to look for him.

20\. FINISH

Dry land! Well done, you've escaped. But what's that sound in the bushes...?

Tauriel

Tauriel is another Elf of Mirkwood and head of the King's Elven Guard. Tauriel is a warrior to be feared and reckoned with. An amazing archer and a skilled swordfighter, she's not someone who you would want to cross. Not if you want to keep your head on your shoulders!

DID YOU KNOW?

In Elvish, Tauriel's name means 'daughter of the forest'.

Tauriel doesn't always follow orders and is very headstrong. When Thranduil orders all of the Elves to stay in Mirkwood after Bilbo and the Dwarves escape, she ignores him and rushes off to follow them to Lake-town.

She is quite unlike other Elves. Tauriel doesn't understand why Thranduil decided to forbid the Wood Elves from becoming involved in what was happening in the rest of Middle-earth, and she also doesn't seem to share the usual Elven dislike of Dwarves.

HIDDEN DANGER

A horde of Mirkwood Spiders are hiding in the trees. Help Thorin and the Dwarves discover their enemies by finding the word spider 21 times in the grid below.

The words can run up, down, diagonally and backwards too.

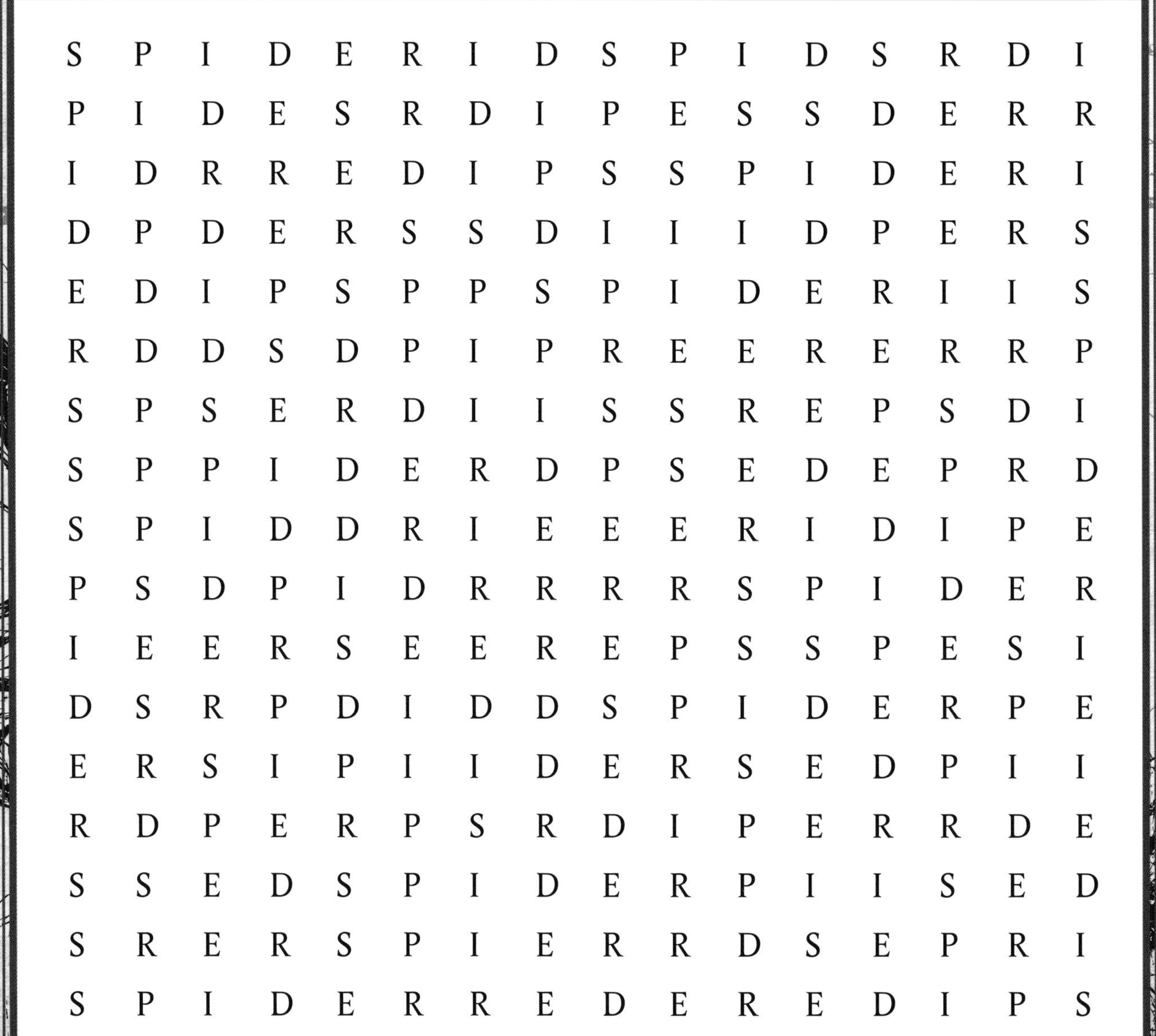

S P I D E R I D S P I D S R D I
P I D E S R D I P E S S D E R R
I D R R E D I P S S P I D E R I
D P D E R S S D I I I D P E R S
E D I P S P P S P I D E R I I S
R D D S D P I P R E E R E R R P
S P S E R D I I S S R E P S D I
S P P I D E R D P S E D E P R D
S P I D D R I E E E R I D I P E
P S D P I D R R R R S P I D E R
I E E R S E E R E P S S P E S I
D S R P D I D D S P I D E R P E
E R S I P I I D E R S E D P I I
R D P E R P S R D I P E R R D E
S S E D S P I D E R P I I S E D
S R E R S P I E R R D S E P R I
S P I D E R R E D E R E D I P S

SURE SHOT

Legolas is a dead-shot with a bow. Help him shoot all the Orcs without hitting Bilbo or the Dwarves.

INSTRUCTIONS

You have 5 arrows in your quiver. Close your eyes and dot a pen on the page 5 times to try and hit the Orcs. How true was your aim?

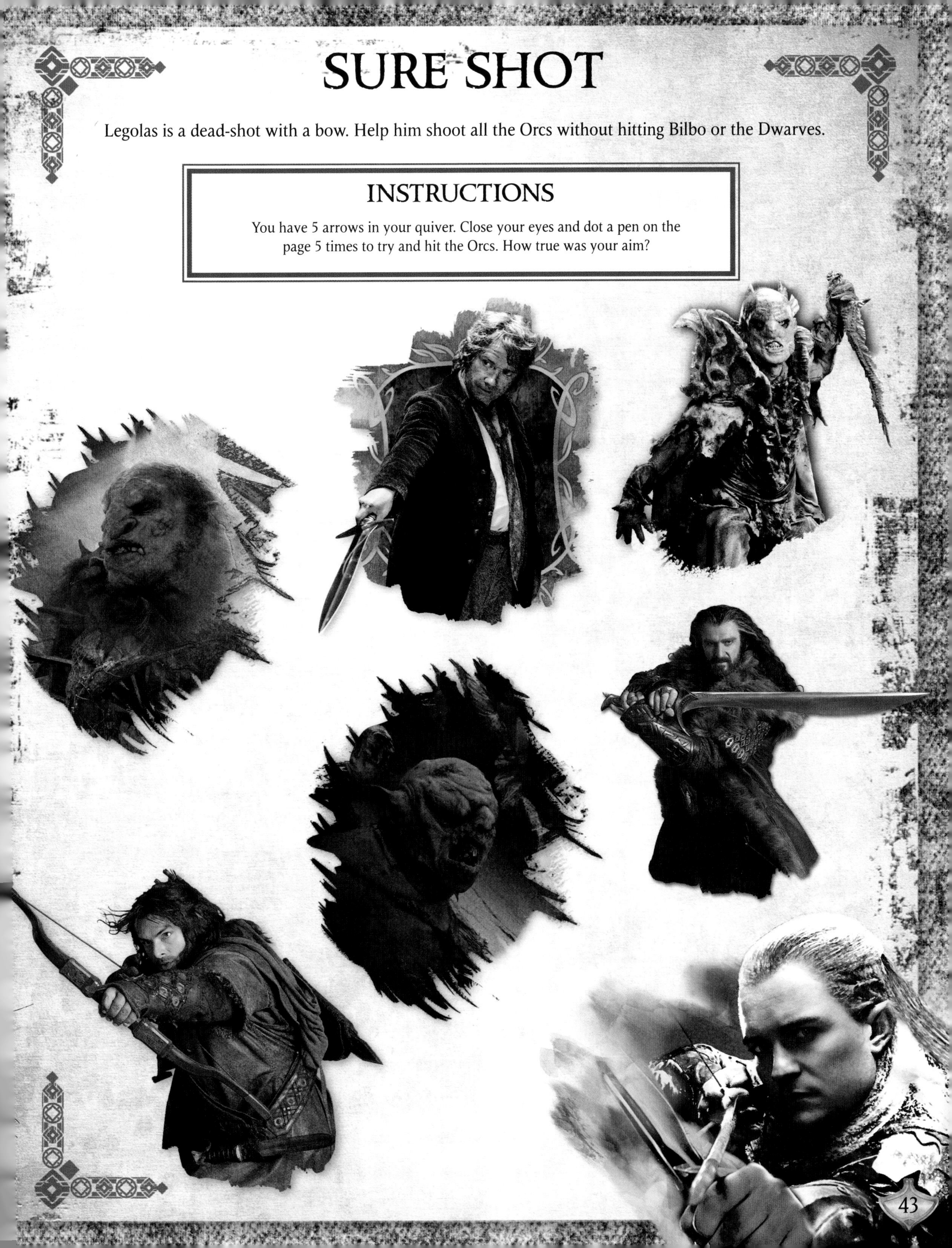

TRICKS AND TRAPS

Gandalf has reached the ruins of Dol Guldur. Pit your wits against the Necromancer's evil puzzles to help Gandalf.

Divide and conquer

The gate is locked. Using only 3 straight lines, divide the carving into 4 areas, each containing 3 runes to open the lock. The areas of the carving can be different sizes and shapes.

Illusion

There is strong magic at work, which is making it hard to believe your own eyes! Look carefully – are the two purple lines straight or curved?

Try getting a ruler to check.

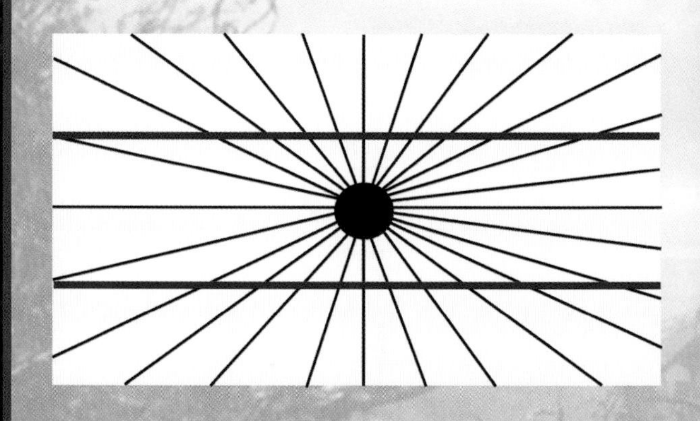

Sure step

The flagstones on the floor are a trap! Read the clues to see in which order Gandalf should step on each flagstone to proceed without setting off the trap.

INSTRUCTIONS

Symbol ᛞ is stepped on immediately after Symbol ᛖ
Symbol ᚨ is always stepped on immediately before Symbol ᛒ.
Symbol ᛒ is always stepped on last.
Symbol ᛚ is stepped on after Symbol ᛞ

SOLUTION

1.
2.
3.
4.
5.

Number spell

Help Gandalf to cast a protection spell by putting these numbers into the missing spaces so that each side of the triangle adds up to 36.

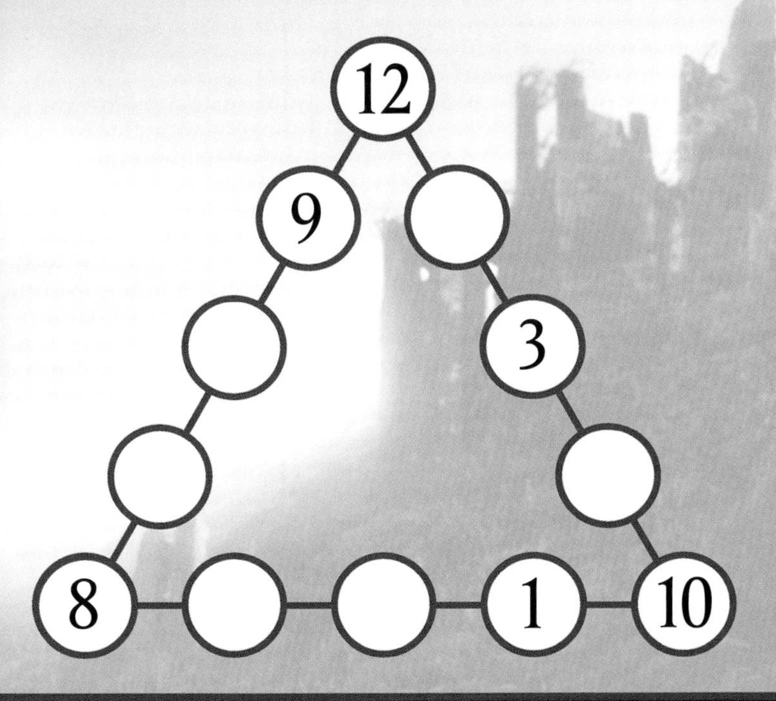

2, 4, 5,
6, 7, 11

The magic number

Look carefully at the image below – how many times can you spot the number 6 in the jumble?

Answer:

SHADOW SEARCH

Bilbo is hunting for Thorin in the dark dungeons of the Hall of the Elven King, but it's so dark he can't see which prisoner is which! Look carefully and see if you can choose the shadow that matches Thorin.

DOUBLE VISION

Gandalf is a master of magic and has created copies of himself to hide from danger. Look closely at the images – can you tell which one is the real Gandalf?

Real Gandalf

A.

B.

C.

D.

E.

F.

BARD

A bargeman from Lake-town, Bard can handle himself in a fight. Fearless and strong, he is a great hunter and often spends his time in the hills around the river leading from Mirkwood into the Long Lake. His weapon of choice is his bow, and he is one of the best archers in all of Middle-earth.

DID YOU KNOW?

Bard has three children: Bain, Sigrid and Tilda.

Bard's path first crosses that of Bilbo and The Company when he finds them washed up ashore after their amazing escape from the halls of the Elven King. To begin with, Bard doesn't trust this strange group of soggy adventurers, but he eventually agrees to help and shows them the way to Lake-town.

DWARF DOODLE

Can you help Ori finish his sketch? Use the grid to copy the picture, square by square, and show off your arty skills.

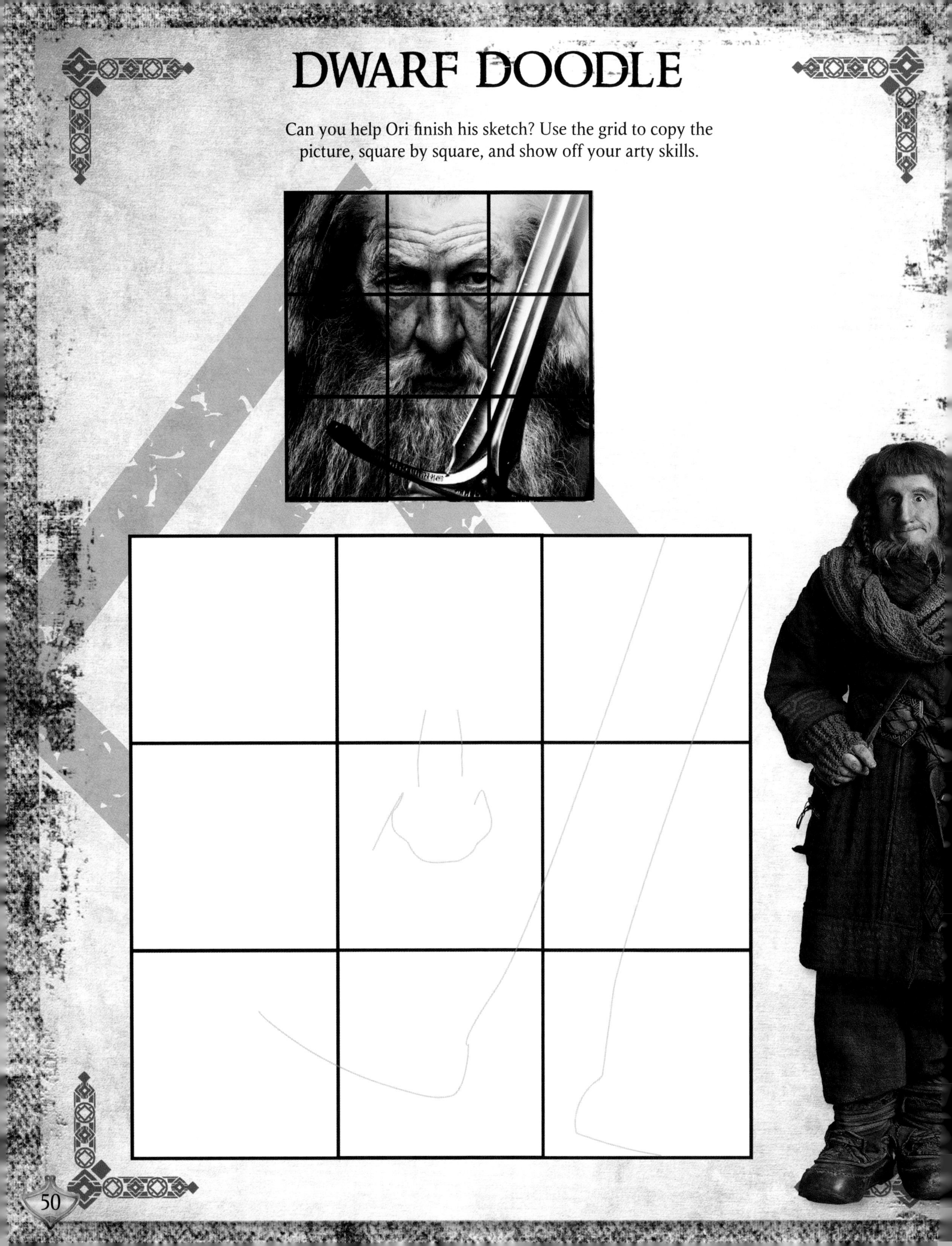

WHAT'S IN A NAME?

Ever wondered what your name would be if you were a Dwarf?
Well, now you can find out!

LIST 1	LIST 2	LIST 3
Take the second letter of your first name:	Take the second letter of your last name:	Take the last letter of your first name:
A: Torin	A: Gray	A: caster
B: Gimtor	B: Spider	B: sword
C: Dathmar	C: Rock	C: shaker
D: Korgen	D: Ground	D: biter
E: Thorthal	E: Silver	E: quake
F: Bakrov	F: Stone	F: breaker
G: Gegrun	G: Mountain	G: axe
H: Birloin	H: Bone	H: smash
I: Gimlorm	I: Bronze	I: helm
J: Doin	J: Iron	J: forger
K: Thoric	K: Earth	K: hammer
L: Hamlin	L: Gem	L: killer
M: Valin	M: Anvil	M: blade
N: Fori	N: Troll	N: crafter
O: Zorin	O: Granite	O: shield
P: Dwori	P: Thunder	P: spike
Q: Barin	Q: Fire	Q: heart
R: Ralnar	R: Gravel	R: carver
S: Morn	S: Flint	S: smith
T: Zakli	T: Flame	T: dagger
U: Tofur	U: Orc	U: crush
V: Himbur	V: Oaken	V: beard
W: Vorn	W: Copper	W: strike
X: Donriz	X: Steam	X: miner
Y: Rolg	Y: Goblin	Y: digger
Z: Bathnar	Z: Blue	Z: hand

Write your Dwarf name here:

MIDDLE-EARTH CREATURES

Middle-earth is not just home to many wondrous races, such as hobbits and Elves, but also to many dangerous and deadly creatures.

GOBLINS

Not much larger than a hobbit, Goblins are actually a kind of Orc. They live in dark caves, clawing out their lives in the slimy shadows. They have extremely good eyesight in the dark and are very good at moving around in narrow tunnels and caves.

For hundreds of years they have spread their evil from within their mountain caves, waging war on Dwarves. Vicious, cunning and completely evil, Goblins are fearsome warriors who rarely take prisoners. More likely to chop you into pieces for their next meal than keep you alive for questioning, they are a danger to Bilbo and his friends.

Goblins smell. Actually, they don't just smell, they stink! But then again if you're that close to a Goblin, how they smell would really be the last thing to worry about!

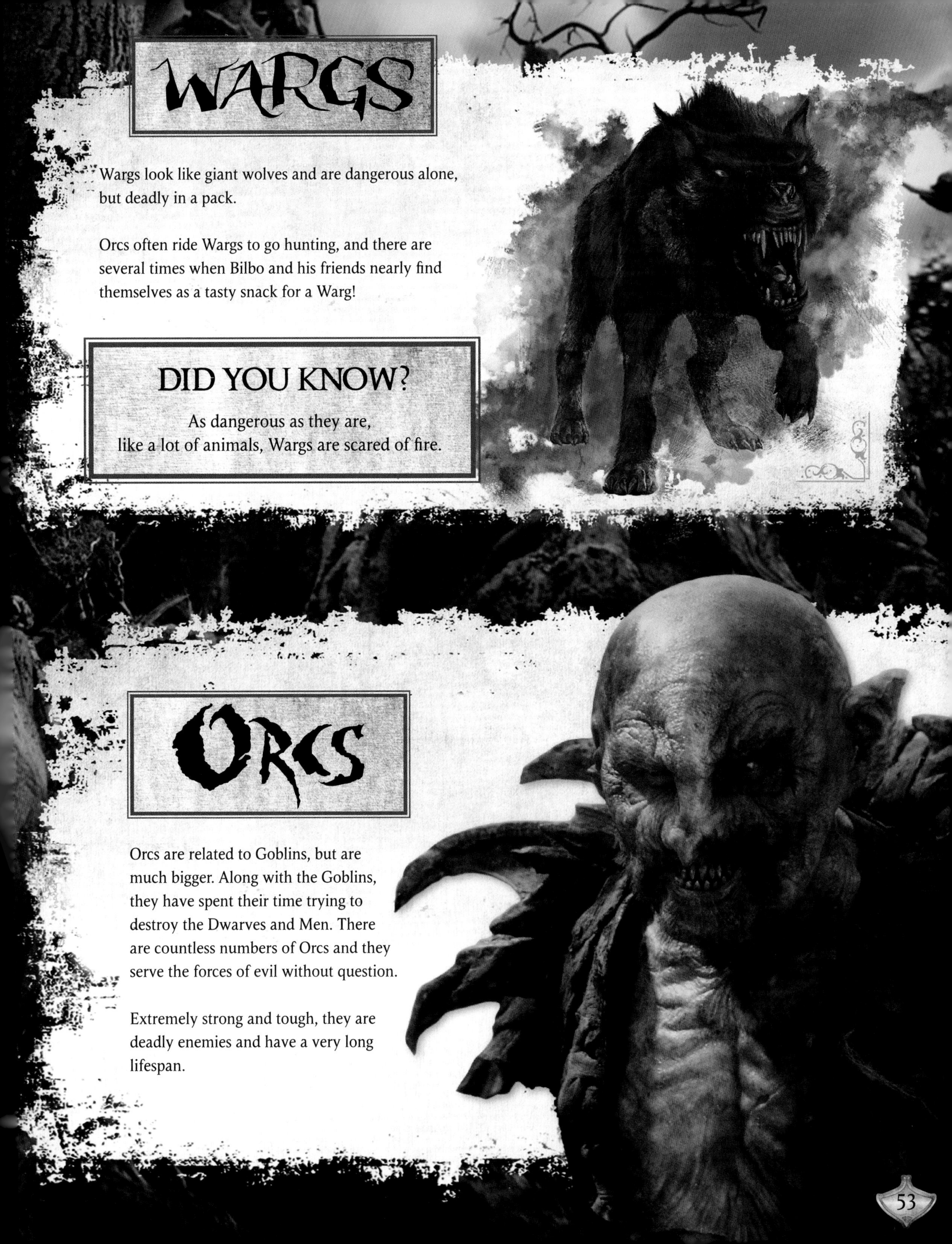

WARGS

Wargs look like giant wolves and are dangerous alone, but deadly in a pack.

Orcs often ride Wargs to go hunting, and there are several times when Bilbo and his friends nearly find themselves as a tasty snack for a Warg!

DID YOU KNOW?

As dangerous as they are,
like a lot of animals, Wargs are scared of fire.

ORCS

Orcs are related to Goblins, but are much bigger. Along with the Goblins, they have spent their time trying to destroy the Dwarves and Men. There are countless numbers of Orcs and they serve the forces of evil without question.

Extremely strong and tough, they are deadly enemies and have a very long lifespan.

CREATURES ASSEMBLE

Can you fit all the creatures from the list, into the grid, below?

Goblin
Necromancer
Orc
Troll
Warg

Once you've filled in the grid, see how many of our heroes' names you can make, using the letters above as many times as you like.

Bilbo	Oin	Thorin
Gandalf	Gloin	Balin
Nori	Bombur	Dwalin
Dori	Bifur	Fili
Ori	Bofur	Kili

COMPANY SPOT

Do you have eyes as sharp as Legolas? Look closely at these two pictures and see if you can spot the 6 differences between them.

A.

B.

Smaug

The scourge of Middle-earth and the bane of the Dwarves, Smaug has spread his foul influence over the whole land for many years. Now, the fearsome Dragon lurks in his lair, jealously guarding his treasure from all who would dare to take it from him. Powerful, magical and pure evil, Smaug is a deadly enemy and a force to be reckoned with.

Years ago, Smaug attacked the legendary home of the Dwarven Kings in the Lonely Mountain. Scorching them with his fiery breath, he drove the Dwarves from their home and scattered them to the four corners of Middle-earth.

Smaug loves treasure and his greed is almost as large as his evil nature. Deep within Erebor, he lies, surrounded by a vast fortune made up of all the gold and jewels left behind by the Dwarves.

One of the most prized pieces of Smaug's treasure is the legendary Arkenstone. It's not only Smaug that desires this fabulous jewel, however – Thorin would do anything to get his hands on it too.

Smaug is a fearsome and seemingly indestructible opponent, covered in scales harder than any armour.

Smaug has an excellent sense of smell and can tell who is near him even in the darkest cavern just by smelling them. However, until Bilbo appears, Smaug had never smelt a hobbit before!

MIDDLE-EARTH MASTERMIND

Think you've learned all there is to know about The Company's quest to the Lonely Mountain? Then take this quiz and prove your expert knowledge.

QUESTION 1:
What animal can Beorn change into?

Boar, bear or bat.

QUESTION 2:
Which of these is not an Elf from Mirkwood?

Tauriel, Legolas, Legolam.

QUESTION 3:
What is the name of the King of the Mirkwood Elves?

Thorin, Thrain, Thranduil.

QUESTION 4:
What do the Dwarves use to escape from the Halls of the Elven King?

Barrels, boxes, benches.

QUESTION 5:
Who is this?

Frodo, Gimli, Ori.

5.

QUESTION 6:
True or False?

The name of the Master's helper is spelled Alfred

QUESTION 7:
Where does Gandalf go to look for evidence of the Necromancer's return?

Lake-town, the Shire, Dol Guldur.

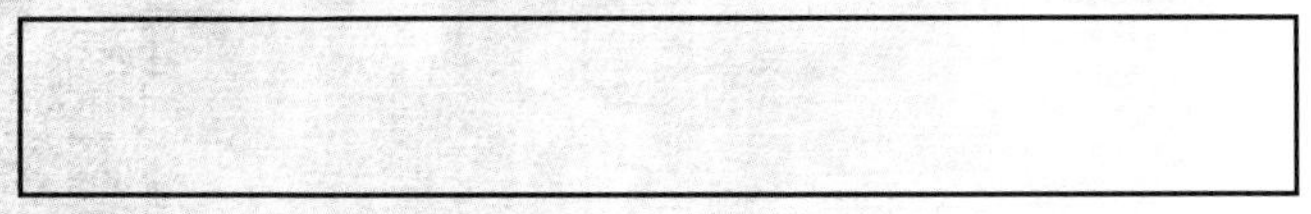

QUESTION 8:
How many Dwarves are in Thorin's Company (including Thorin himself)?

12, 13 or 14.

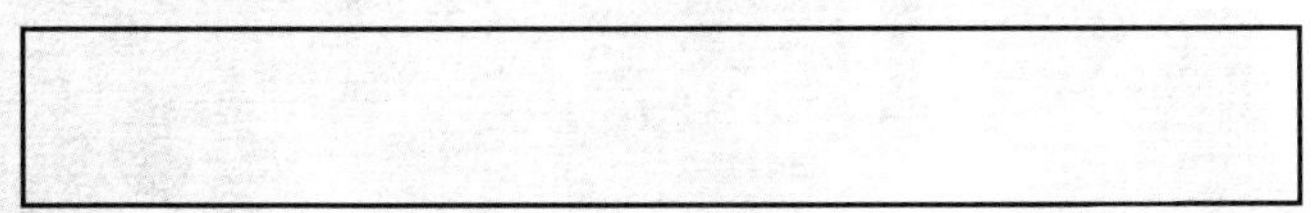

QUESTION 9:
What kind of creatures captured the Dwarves
when they strayed from the path in Mirkwood??

Wargs, Goblins, spiders.

QUESTION 10:
True or False?

Bard has three children.

Tauriel
daughter of Mirkwood
Legolas
Greenleaf

ANSWERS

pages 16-17
TATTERED AND TORN

A=4, B=2, C=6, D=7.

page 18
DESPERATE DASH

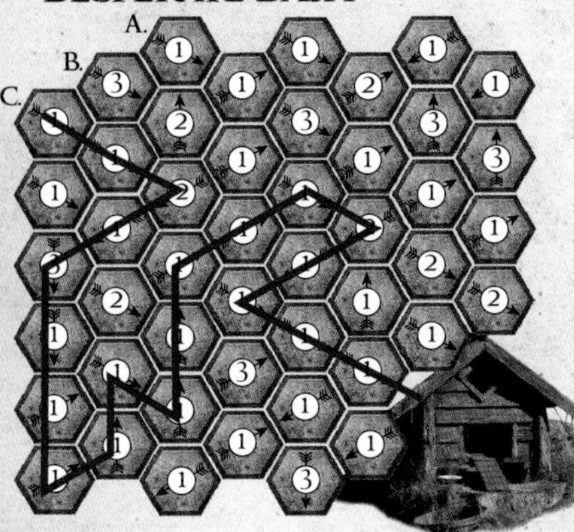

page 19
RUNE WHEEL

The message is:
THE BEAR IS BEORN.

page 26
RUNE REMEDIES

Puzzle 1.

Puzzle 2.

Puzzle 3.

ᚨ	ᛞ	ᛒ	ᛚ
ᛚ	ᛒ	ᛞ	ᚨ
ᛞ	ᚨ	ᛚ	ᛒ
ᛒ	ᛚ	ᚨ	ᛞ

pages 28-29
SPIDER SEARCH

pages 30-31
MIRKWOOD MUDDLERS

The power of 5.

START	1+3	21÷3	90÷30	45÷5	26-23	18-15	9÷3
4x2	10-6	18-12	24-17	60-54	40÷10	2×3	2+2
23-17	2x2	9-6	1x4	17-11	9-7	1+5	100÷25
40÷20	6+5	5+4	8÷2	30-26	21÷7	8÷1	3×1
3×9	11-6	22÷2	34-27	9-3	20÷2	14×2	FINISH

Shape-shifting.
A.=22, B.=18, C.=21, D=24.
The ring is in pocket D.

Number tree.

48 [96] 48
22 19 [82] 19 22
8 14 5 [54] 5 14 8
6 9 7 1 46 1 7 9 6

Take aim.
A and C

page 34
DUNGEON RUNNER

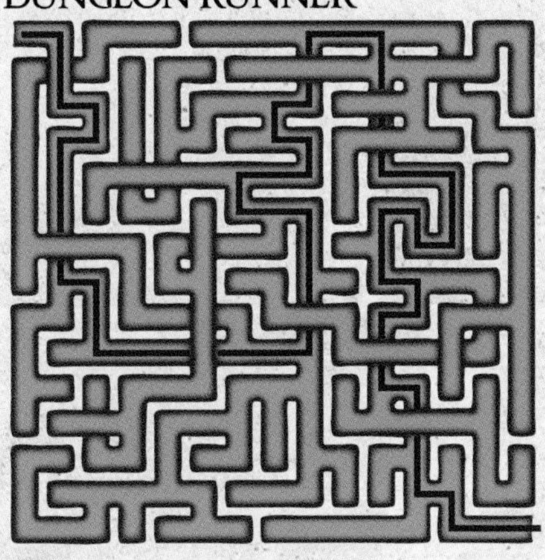

page 36
BARREL BOTHER

Bofur=D, Dori=C, Kili=B, Bifur=E, Nori=A.

page 37
SPOT THE DIFFERENCE

page 42
HIDDEN DANGER

S	P	I	D	E	R	I	D	S	P	I	D	S	R	D	I
P	I	D	E	S	R	D	I	P	E	S	S	D	E	R	R
I	D	R	R	E	D	I	P	S	S	P	I	D	E	R	I
D	P	D	E	R	S	S	D	I	I	I	D	P	E	R	S
E	D	I	P	S	P	P	S	P	I	D	E	R	I	I	S
R	D	D	S	D	P	I	P	R	E	E	R	E	R	R	P
S	P	S	E	R	D	I	I	S	S	R	E	P	S	D	I
S	P	P	I	D	E	R	D	P	S	E	D	E	P	R	D
S	P	I	D	D	R	I	E	E	E	R	I	D	I	P	E
P	S	D	P	I	D	R	R	R	R	S	P	I	D	E	R
I	E	E	R	S	E	E	R	E	P	S	S	P	E	S	I
D	S	R	P	D	I	D	D	S	P	I	D	E	R	P	E
E	R	S	I	P	I	I	D	E	R	S	E	D	P	I	I
R	D	P	E	R	P	S	R	D	I	P	E	R	R	D	E
S	S	E	D	S	P	I	D	E	R	P	I	I	S	E	D
S	R	E	R	S	P	I	E	R	R	D	S	E	P	R	I
S	P	I	D	E	R	R	E	D	E	R	E	D	I	P	S

pages 44-45
TRICKS AND TRAPS

Divide and conquer

Illusion

The purple lines are straight

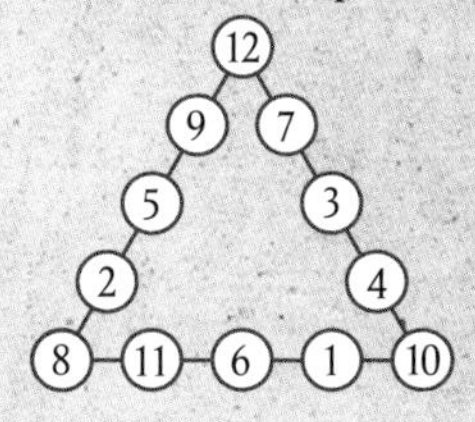

Sure step

1. Symbol ᛗ
2. Symbol ᛞ
3. Symbol ᛚ
4. Symbol ᚨ
5. Symbol ᛒ

Number spell

12
9 7
5 3
2 4
8–11–6–1–10

The magic number
There are eight 6s.

page 46
SHADOW SEARCH

Shadow G matches Thorin.

page 47
DOUBLE VISION

C is the real Gandalf.

page 54
CREATURES ASSEMBLE

								O		
				G		W		R		T
N	E	C	R	O	M	A	N	C	E	R
				B		R				O
				L		G				L
				I						L
				N						

The names you can make are:
Bilbo, Nori, Ori, Oin, Gloin and Balin.

page 55
COMPANY SPOT

pages 58-59
MIDDLE-EARTH MASTERMIND

1. Bear, 2. Legolam, 3. Thranduil
4. Barrels, 5. Ori, 6. False. It's Alfrid,
7. Dol Guldur, 8. 13, 9. Spiders, 10. True

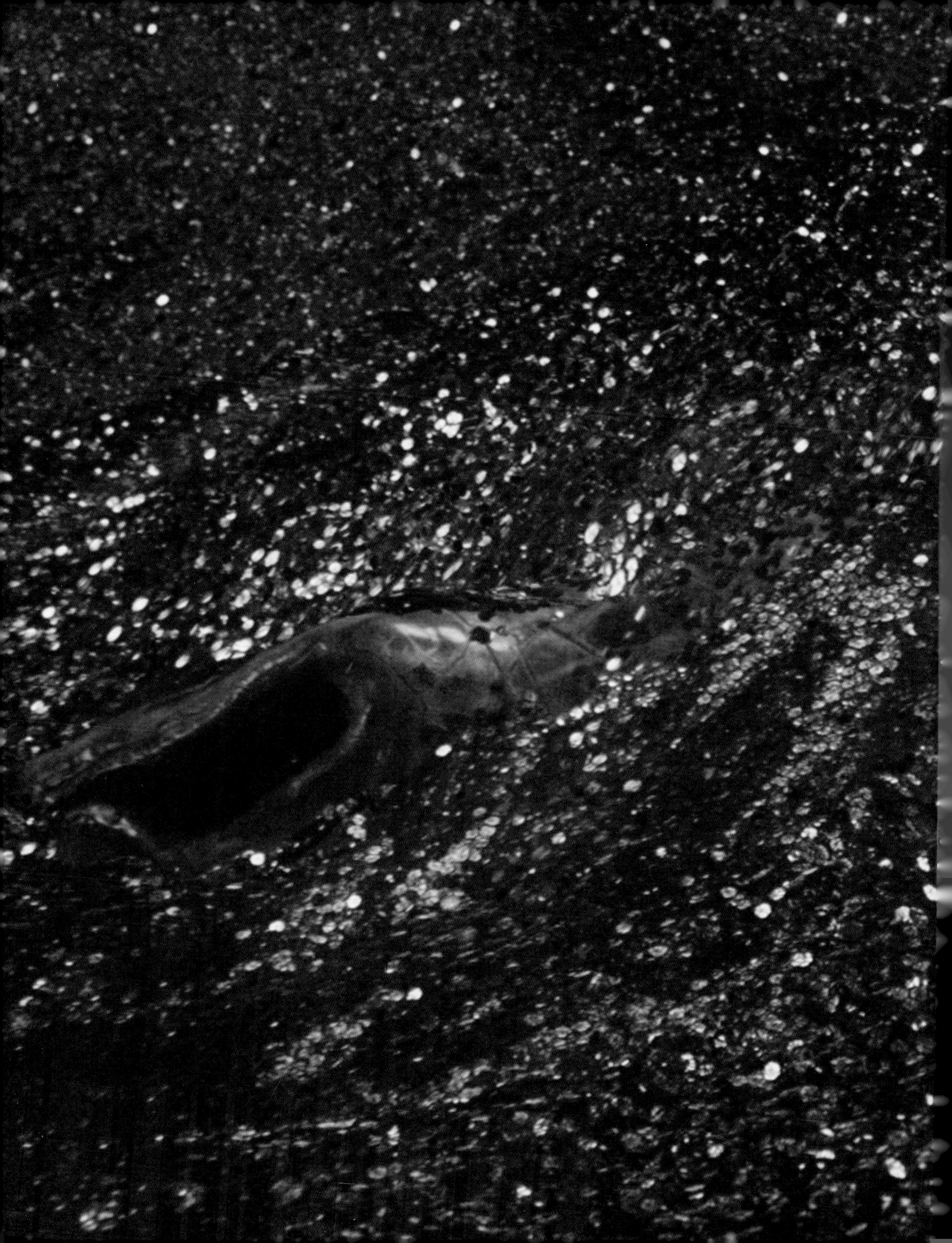